"I DON'T LIKE CHOOSE YOUR OWN ADVENTURE® BOOKS. I *LOVE* THEM!" says Jessica Gordon, age ten. And now kids between the ages of six and nine can choose their own adventures too. Here's what kids have to say about the Skylark Choose Your Own Adventure® books.

"These are my favorite books because you can pick whatever choice you want— and the story is all about you."
—**Katy Alson,** *age 8*

"I love finding out how my story will end."
—**Joss Williams,** *age 9*

"I like all the illustrations!"
—**Savitri Brightfield,** *age 7*

"A six-year-old friend and I have lots of fun making the decisions together."
—**Peggy Marcus** *(adult)*

Bantam Skylark Books in the Choose Your Own Adventure®
  Series
Ask your bookseller for the books you have missed

#1 THE CIRCUS
#2 THE HAUNTED HOUSE
#3 SUNKEN TREASURE
#4 YOUR VERY OWN ROBOT
#5 GORGA, THE SPACE MONSTER
#6 THE GREEN SLIME
#7 HELP! YOU'RE SHRINKING
#8 INDIAN TRAIL
#9 DREAM TRIPS
#10 THE GENIE IN THE BOTTLE
#11 THE BIGFOOT MYSTERY
#12 THE CREATURE FROM MILLER'S POND
#13 JUNGLE SAFARI
#14 THE SEARCH FOR CHAMP
#15 THE THREE WISHES
#16 DRAGONS!
#17 WILD HORSE COUNTRY
#18 SUMMER CAMP
#19 THE TOWER OF LONDON
#20 TROUBLE IN SPACE
#21 MONA IS MISSING
#22 THE EVIL WIZARD
#23 THE POLAR BEAR EXPRESS
#24 THE MUMMY'S TOMB
#25 THE FLYING CARPET
#26 THE MAGIC PATH
#27 ICE CAVE
#28 FIRE!
#29 THE FAIRY KIDNAP
#30 RUNAWAY SPACESHIP
#31 LOST DOG!
#32 BLIZZARD AT BLACK SWAN INN
#33 HAUNTED HARBOR
#34 ATTACK OF THE MONSTER PLANTS
#35 THE MISS LIBERTY CAPER
#36 THE OWL TREE

THE OWL TREE

R.A. MONTGOMERY

ILLUSTRATED BY LESLIE MORRILL

A BANTAM SKYLARK BOOK®
TORONTO · NEW YORK · LONDON · SYDNEY · AUCKLAND

RL 2, 007–009

THE OWL TREE
A Bantam Skylark Book / September 1986

CHOOSE YOUR OWN ADVENTURE® is a registered trademark of Bantam Books, Inc.

Original conception of Edward Packard.

Skylark Books is a registered trademark of Bantam Books, Inc. Registered in U.S. Patent and Trademark Office and elsewhere.

ISBN 0-553-15449-4

Published simultaneously in the United States and Canada

Bantam Books are published by Bantam Books, Inc. Its trademark, consisting of the words "Bantam Books" and the portrayal of a rooster, is Registered in U.S. Patent and Trademark Office and in other countries. Marca Registrada. Bantam Books, Inc., 666 Fifth Avenue, New York, New York 10103.

PRINTED IN THE UNITED STATES OF AMERICA

CW   0 9 8 7 6 5 4 3 2 1

To Shannon P. Gilligan

READ THIS FIRST!!!

Most books are about other people.

This book is about you! What happens to you at the owl tree depends on what you decide to do.

Do not read this book from the first page through to the last page. Instead, start on page one and read until you come to your first choice. Then turn to the page shown and see what happens.

When you come to the end of a story, go back and start again. Every choice leads to a new adventure.

Good luck, and beware of magic owls who try to trick you!

The day you discovered the owl tree was **1** magical. You were hiking in the forest near your house when you stumbled into a large clearing. In the center of it stood a maple tree. Its trunk was so thick that four kids linking hands would barely circle it!

As you stood under the tree looking up, you were surprised by several questions.

"Whooo?"

"Whoooo?"

"Whoooooo?"

"It's me," you replied, wondering who was asking, "who?"

Then a bunch of owls poked their heads out of the tree. You spent the day there and learned many of the owls' secrets.

Turn to page 3.

Today your best friend, Sally, is coming to **3** the owl tree with you. It's a sunny Saturday— a perfect day for a hike in the woods. You lace up your hiking boots, strap on your backpack, and head for the corner of your street where Sally is waiting.

When the two of you reach the clearing, you stand still. Softly you call, *"Whooo? Whooo?"* Minutes later some owls pop out of the tree.

"What happens now?" asks Sally.

"We can follow an owl to a magic kingdom," you say. "But we'll have to wait until one leaves."

"What's the other choice?" she asks.

"We can ask the owls some questions. They're very wise."

"You decide," Sally answers. "You've been here before."

If you wait and follow an owl to a magic kingdom, turn to page 7.

If you decide to ask the owls questions, turn to page 8.

4   "I see something moving over there," you say, pointing to the trail. "Let's go that way."

You and Sally follow the trail for awhile. Along the way you spot a strange-looking bush with two bright yellow flowers. As you step toward it there's a flash of wings. Two bright yellow *eyes*—not flowers—blink at you! It's the owl!

With a loud hoot he flies off above the trail. You and Sally follow as best you can on the ground.

Finally the owl makes a left by an oak tree, and you round the corner after him. You don't see the owl anywhere, but hanging from a birch tree is a plump leather sack.

If you decide to look in the sack, turn to page 18.

If you decide to keep looking for the owl, turn to page 14.

6 "Bring me fresh raspberries from the bushes of Illnoor," the saw-whet owl replies, blinking his eyes.

"What's Illnoor?" you ask.

"It's the home of the Great Zoonies. They are large and very mean creatures. They guard the raspberry bushes."

"That sounds dangerous!" Sally snaps. Then she turns to you. "I'm not going anywhere. Are you going to Illnoor?"

If you travel alone to Illnoor,
turn to page 23.

If you tell the owl you won't go,
turn to page 15.

You and Sally settle down to wait. The forest floor is soft and the day is warm. The owls watch you. They swivel their heads back and forth and blink their huge eyes.

Suddenly a barn owl leaves with a flap of wings.

"One's leaving," you shout. "Let's go."

Turn to page 12.

8   You step close to the owl tree and ask in your most polite voice, "Oh, owls, most wise owls, what will I be when I grow up?"

A small saw-whet owl leans forward and speaks in a whisper. "If you are prepared to carry out my every command, then I will reveal your future."

"Forget it, owl," Sally says. "I have enough commands to obey. My big brother bosses me around all the time!"

You don't know what to do. Who knows what this owl will command? Maybe you can get one of the other owls to answer your question.

If you ask the saw-whet owl what he wants you to do, turn to page 6.

If you ask a different owl about your future, turn to page 20.

"I thought I saw him on the other side of the **11** river. Let's try to cross it," you say.

You look for a way to get to the other side. Luckily, there's an old wooden boat pulled up on the bank. The oars are still in it.

"Let's borrow the boat," you say.

"Maybe we shouldn't. It's not ours," Sally says.

"This boat hasn't been used in a long time. Look at all the leaves in the bottom," you reply. "We can return it after we find the owl."

The two of you push the boat into the river and jump aboard. You begin to row across. But the river is flowing very fast and the boat gets caught in its swift current.

"Help, Sally! I can't control the boat!" you yell.

Turn to page 24.

12   You and Sally take off after the owl. The forest is thick with trees and plants. The owl soars above them, dipping in and out of view. As you run you trip over roots and stumble over bushes.

Suddenly you come to a wide river. You look up, but the owl is gone! To the right of the river is a well-used trail. On your left stands a high stone wall. It looks old and crumbly.

"Drats!" you say to Sally. "Which way should we go?"

If you decide to cross the river,
turn to page 11.

If you decide to climb over the wall,
turn to page 17.

If you decide to follow the trail,
turn to page 4.

14   You turn toward the forest—the owl may have gone that way. But Sally stays right where she is. "I want to look in the sack," she says. "I'll catch up with you later."

You follow a muddy trail for a short while. But as you hike deeper into the woods, moss and large tree roots sprawl over the path. And the trees and bushes become thicker, blocking out the sun. Your heart races a little—it's pretty dark here!

You hike about half a mile, but there's still no sign of the owl. You lean against a tree and close your eyes. You rest for a few minutes. But suddenly you hear some leaves rustle, and then another noise—like footsteps.

Turn to page 27.

When you refuse to go to Illnoor, the saw-whet owl stares hard at you. He looks mad, but you don't care. You're not about to change your mind!

Finally the owl winks at you and Sally. Then he says, "I was just testing you. You've responded wisely to my request. So, now I'll tell you what the future holds. Ready?"

You yell, "Ready!" The owl shifts his feathers.

Turn to page 35.

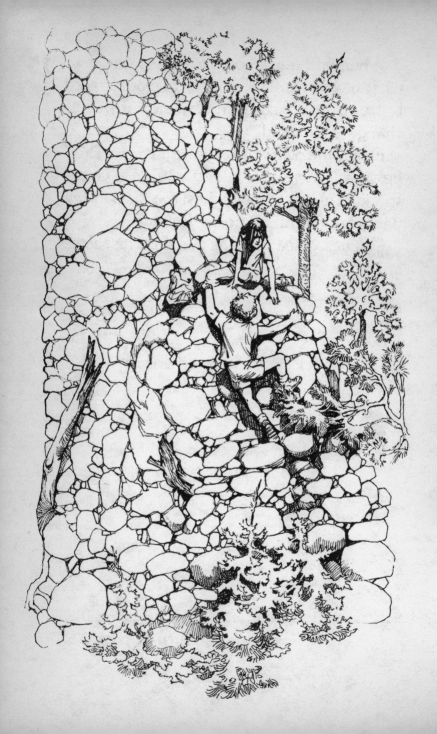

You and Sally each grab hold of a sturdy **17** stone in the wall and pull yourselves up. You manage to climb about three feet from the bottom. But when you look up, you see that the top of the wall isn't getting any closer. Then it hits you: As you climb it, this old stone wall is *growing*!

"I don't think we're getting anywhere," Sally shouts. "What do you think we should do?"

If you say, "Let's jump off this wall," turn to page 28.

If you say, "Let's keep trying to climb this old wall," turn to page 39.

18   You shinny up the trunk of the birch tree and crawl along a thin white branch. As you reach for the sack you hear the branch bend.

"Watch out!" Sally cries.

Crack! Wham! Thud!

The sack, branch, and *you* fall to the ground!

You're not hurt, but the sack is. There's a long rip down the middle. A strange light spills from the tear and spreads on the ground like a puddle of water.

Turn to page 41.

20   You look up at a horned owl. "Oh, horned owl, you look wiser than the little saw-whet owl. Can *you* tell me what I'll be when I grow up?"

The horned owl clears his throat. He's about to answer you when the small saw-whet owl speaks up.

"Just wait one minute, my friend! I'm just as wise—or wiser! I'll prove it too. Ask me another question."

You can't decide. Should you ask the saw-whet owl the same question or try a new one?

If you ask the same question,
turn to page 32.

If you ask a different question,
turn to page 42.

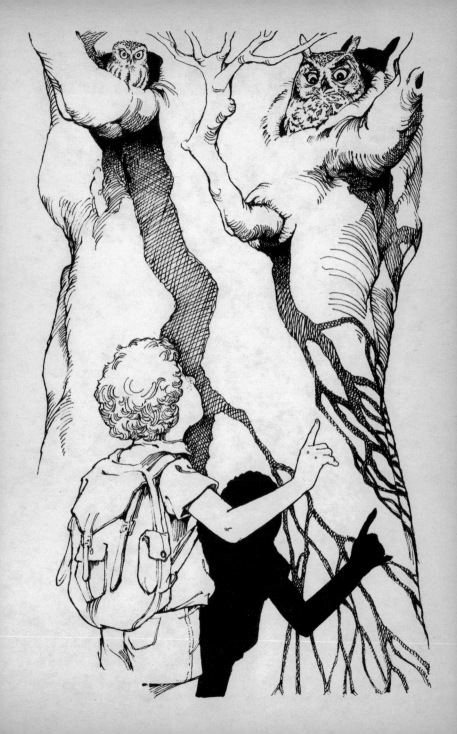

It doesn't take long to get to Illnoor. From a distance you can see the Great Zoonies and they look harmless. They're furry creatures shaped like caterpillars—only bigger.

Turn to page 45.

24 Just then the barn owl flies overhead.

"Took on a bit too much today, I see," he says in a squeaky voice.

"He *talks*!" Sally shouts, so surprised that she almost falls over the side of the boat.

"Please help us, owl," you beg. "This boat is out of control!"

"Go with the current and aim for shore when you get close to the bank of the river," the owl replies wisely. "You'll be safe."

Your boat bounces in the rough water while you watch the owl fly away. Finally the river bends, and you use the oars to steer the boat toward the bank. It bumps up on a sandy beach.

"I don't know about you, Sally," you say as you climb out of the boat, "but *I* think home will look like a magic kingdom after this boat ride!"

The End

Who's coming? you wonder nervously. It **27** may be Sally catching up to you. On the other hand it could be something dangerous—like a bear looking for dinner!

If you think it's Sally and stay where you are, turn to page 31.

If you break into a run, turn to page 36.

28   Just as you and Sally are about to drop to the ground, the barn owl lands on top of the wall. He peers down at you.

"Too late, too late," he says. "You should have tried to climb to the top of the wall. I would have shown you the Castle of Remembrance where dreams stay alive. We would have visited the Hall of Flowers where spring and summer never end. Oh well, maybe we'll visit another day."

Then the owl disappears and the stone wall shrinks. To the west you see the sun sinking behind the trees. It's too late today for any more exploring, but you'll go back to the owl tree another day!

The End

You stand up straight against the tree and **31** wait for whomever, or whatever, is coming. You hope it's Sally!

The footsteps sound closer and closer. Finally a clump of bushes parts, and Sally steps through it! Her face is red with excitement.

"Boy, am I glad to see you," you say.

"Never mind that," she says. "Look at what I found in the sack." She puts something heavy into your hand.

Turn to page 50.

32 "What am I going to be when I grow up?" you ask for the second time. You wait patiently while the owl stretches to his full height. He rearranges his feathers. He blinks his eyes. Finally he speaks.

"That's a difficult question. A very difficult question. You could be a teacher or a writer or a doctor or a lawyer or an artist or a builder or anything you want to be. You'll have to wait and find out."

The saw-whet owl hoots good-bye as he and the other owls duck back into the owl tree. As you and Sally hike home through the forest, you think about the owl's answer. You wish he told you more about your future, but you know he's right—what happens is up to you!

The End

The owl rolls his round eyes.

"The world will survive. There will be hard times and even dangerous times, but the world will survive. You must help it, though."

How will you help?

The End

Suddenly a bigger saw-whet owl swoops out of the owl tree.

"Okay, Sammy. That's enough for today," she says. "Stop teasing those humans."

The small saw-whet owl disappears into a hole in the owl tree. Then the larger one looks at you and Sally and says, "Owls are very wise, but we can't tell the future!"

The End

36   You run as fast as you can. You are out of breath when you get back to the birch tree. Sally is crawling along one of its branches.

"Hello," she cries. "You're white as a ghost. Did the owl scare you?"

"I thought you might need some help back here," you say quickly. There's no need to explain that you just ran away from a noise!

Sally reaches for the sack. But before she can grab it, it shakes loose from the branch. Suddenly it has wings. . . . The sack is a horned owl!

The owl circles overhead and then rests on a branch. "Why have you entered *my* forest?" he demands.

Turn to page 47.

You and Sally back away from the wall and **39** begin to count.

"One . . . two . . . three . . . GO!"

And suddenly you're both sitting on top of it—almost as if you flew!

When you look down over the wall, you see a castle surrounded by an old-fashioned town. Tiny people are running around busily. Some are adding bricks to a fort outside the castle. Others are hooking up horses to carts.

"It's the Kingdom of Gollop," says a calm voice beside you.

Turn to page 44.

"Sallllly. Sallllllllyyy!" you say in a frightened whisper. She is hiding behind you.

"What is that stuff?" she asks.

At that very moment the light gathers together, rises off the ground, and swirls into a cloudy shape. Slowly the figure of a creature—half owl, half deer—appears.

"I am the spirit of this forest. I rule the birds, the wind, the sky, the sunlight, the rain, and all the animals. I will grant you one wish. What will it be?" The creature waits for you to answer.

What is your wish?

The End

42   You decide to ask the owl a new question. You huddle with Sally. Finally you speak up.

"Oh, wise and great saw-whet owl, what will happen to the world?"

There is silence. You can hear yourself breathe and the tree's leaves gently rubbing together.

Turn to page 33.

44   The barn owl is sitting on the wall next to you!

"It's a shame you can't visit Gollop right now," the owl continues. "The Gollops are getting ready to battle the Evil Fotons."

But before you ask the owl more about Gollop and the Evil Fotons, the wall shrinks to its normal size and the kingdom disappears. The owl is gone.

Turn to page 48.

When you enter Illnoor the Great Zoonies welcome you and invite you to a feast of raspberries. After you stuff yourself with the juicy berries, you rest in the warm sun. You explain to the Great Zoonies why you've come. They tell you that the saw-whet owl always tries to *steal* the raspberries. "If only he'd ask," one says with a sigh. "We'd give him all the berries he wanted."

You decide to stay with the Great Zoonies. From time to time you miss Sally and your family. And you wonder if the saw-whet owl is still waiting for you. But you no longer need the owl's wisdom. Now you know that your future will be a happy life in Illnoor!

The End

Quickly you step forward. "We're sorry, Mr. **47** Owl—if you are a mister owl. We didn't mean to trespass. We didn't hurt anything, honest."

"*Harumph!* A likely story," he responds. "Well, get going. This is *my* forest, and I say out. Now!"

"Let's go home," you say to Sally. "*Whooo* knows what this mean old owl will do!"

The End

48 "I guess we're not going to see a magic kingdom today," you say to Sally as you jump down from the wall. "Let's head back to the owl tree and see if we can get the owls to answer some questions."

When you get back to the tree several owls are sitting in its branches.

Turn to page 8.

50   You look at what Sally has given you. It's a long gold bar and carved into it are the words:

ADMIT TWO TO THE KINGDOM OF GOLLOP.

"The Kingdom of Gollop," you say. "That's a secret kingdom. One of the owls told me about it when I found the owl tree."

Then you look up. The barn owl is circling over your heads. "Come on, owl!" you shout. "Lead the way to Gollop!"

The End

ABOUT THE AUTHOR

R.A. Montgomery is an educator and publisher. A graduate of Williams College, he also studied in graduate programs at Yale University and New York University. After serving in a variety of administrative capacities at Williston Academy and Columbia University, he co-founded the Waitsfield Summer School in 1965. Following that, Montgomery helped found a research and development firm specializing in the development of educational programs. He worked for several years as a consultant to the Peace Corps in Washington, D.C., and West Africa. He is now both a writer and a publisher.

ABOUT THE ILLUSTRATOR

Leslie Morrill is a designer and illustrator whose work has won him numerous awards. He has illustrated over thirty books for children, including the Bantam Classics edition of *The Wind in the Willows*; for the Bantam Skylark Choose Your Own Adventure series, *Indian Trail, Mona Is Missing,* and *Attack of the Monster Plants*; and for the Choose Your Own Adventure series, *Lost on the Amazon, Mountain Survival,* and *Danger at Anchor Mine*. His work has also appeared frequently in *Cricket* magazine. A graduate of the Boston Museum School of Fine Arts, Mr. Morrill lives near Boston, Massachusetts.

CHOOSE YOUR OWN ADVENTURE

SKYLARK EDITIONS

☐	15480	The Green Slime #6 S. Saunders	$2.25
☐	15195	Help! You're Shrinking #7 E. Packard	$1.95
☐	15201	Indian Trail #8 R. A. Montgomery	$1.95
☐	15190	Dream Trips #9 E. Packard	$1.95
☐	15191	The Genie In the Bottle #10 J. Razzi	$1.95
☐	15222	The Big Foot Mystery #11 L. Sonberg	$1.95
☐	15424	The Creature From Millers Pond #12 S. Saunders	$2.25
☐	15226	Jungle Safari #13 E. Packard	$1.95
☐	15442	The Search For Champ #14 S. Gilligan	$2.25
☐	15444	Three Wishes #15 S. Gilligan	$2.25
☐	15465	Dragons! #16 J. Razzi	$2.25
☐	15261	Wild Horse Country #17 L. Sonberg	$1.95
☐	15262	Summer Camp #18 J. Gitenstein	$1.95
☐	15270	The Tower of London #19 S. Saunders	$1.95
☐	15271	Trouble In Space #20 J. Woodcock	$1.95
☐	15283	Mona Is Missing #21 S. Gilligan	$1.95
☐	15418	The Evil Wizard #22 A. Packard	$2.25
☐	15305	The Flying Carpet #25 J. Razzi	$1.95
☐	15318	The Magic Path #26 J. Goodman	$1.95
☐	15467	Ice Cave #27 Saunders, Packard	$2.25
☐	15342	The Fairy Kidnap #29 S. Gilligan	$1.95
☐	15463	Runaway Spaceship #30 S. Saunders	$2.25
☐	15356	Lost Dog! #31 R. A. Montgomery	$1.95
☐	15379	Blizzard of Black Swan #32 Saunders/Packard	$2.25
☐	15380	Haunted Harbor #33 S. Gilligan	$2.25
☐	15399	Attack of the Monster Plants #34 S. Saunders	$2.25

Prices and availability subject to change without notice.